GOD'S PURPOSE

BY

FELICIA GREEN

AUTHOR'S NOTE

I have been helping people for quite some time now and its fun! I love doing this; I love how it brings the life out of me. For the rest of my life, I see myself doing this, and, when the curtain comes down on my life, I would have touched as many people through my writing and speaking.

I can safely say the above is my purpose. Just reading the statement alone tells how excited I get about what I do, and it also tells you that I am going to be doing this for the rest of my life.

As such, you are to serve your purpose for the rest of your life. There must not be a point when you sit back, and declare that you have done enough, or touched enough souls over time. There are just no reservations when it comes to serving your purpose. It's more like your God's calling, and thus, should be lived by until the end of time.

In this book, I teach you how to remain purposeful throughout your life. With the tittle, I chose the words, "Gods Purpose" because life is full of as many surprises, twists, and turns which are not always pleasant. When this happen, most people give up, or forget where they are supposed to be headed. They end up leaving their purposes hanging in exchange for following the wind.

After reading this, I believe you will understand that you have a purpose to serve, and that it must be protected at all cost. I also believe that many who are not sure of what they should call their purpose would have had some light as soon as they finish reading.

I am glad to be taking you through the self-development path, let's hold each other's hands as we strive to build better communities, and eventually a better world, because communities are the ones that feed into countries, and countries into the rest of the world.

TABLE OF CONTENTS

INTRODUCTION

A purposeful life is fun; it gives you the reason to live. Did you know that God created you for a special purpose? Everyone has their own, and the responsibility lies on their shoulders to look around for it. With some, it takes time to discover where it is exactly, but with others, the answers are readily available.

God's purpose is more than your own sense of security and safety that you are after. You could be constantly pursuing your happiness and pleasure, there is nothing wrong with that, but you were created for something better and bigger than that. You were created for God's pleasure that is found in his purpose. Finding the purpose is part of the process, and fulfilling it completes the whole reason why you are here on earth. Defeat is only but a temporary condition; only giving up makes it permanent. For you to find satisfaction and fulfilment, you should live on God's purpose and not give up.

Life is challenging sometimes. The unexpected sometimes happens; you may experience relationship challenges with family and friends, financial stress, health complications, loss of loved ones among other difficult challenges. You may also be affected by economic, social and political challenges. These life challenges may drain, frustrate and discourage you, finding it hard to believe in and pursuing God's purpose over your life. The difficulties of life can leave you wondering where God is, leaving you at the brink of giving up. It is easy to follow the Lord when everything is okay. The real test comes when you go through a rough patch.

God's purpose is bigger than your challenges. He has something great in store for your life. He has good intentions for your life and he doesn't intend to have you struggle through life all the time. He does not promise roses on your bed every time either, challenging times will come your way. James encourages us to approach challenges with positivity, "Consider it pure joy, my brothers and sisters, whenever you face trials of many kinds, because you know that the testing of your faith produces perseverance. Let perseverance finish its work so that you may be mature and complete, not lacking anything." James 1:2-4. You should consider it pure joy when you are faced with different life challenges because your faith will bring you out of the challenge with maturity in God and completeness.

God is omnipresent, which means He is everywhere. He is right there with you as you hit your rock bottom. Even though sometimes you can't feel him, and feel like all hope is gone. God promised to never leave you nor forsake you. His presence is not limited by your feelings. He wants you to have faith and trust him more than anything else. Some of the situations you will face will stretch your faith and leave you wanting to give up. Consider the story of Job, he lost everything he ever owned, his children, health and wealth. People dear to him even told him to give up on God, but he kept on believing God. Life challenges should never be the reason for you to give up on God and His purpose for your life.

You should find comfort in God's promise that he is always with you. He will never leave nor forsake you. When you find yourself discouraged, frustrated and about to give up, remember that God is right there with you. When he is not working on your situation he is usually working on you. He could be working on your attitude, thoughts and faith for His own will and purpose.

Apostle Paul writes, "We know that in all things God works for good with those who love him, those whom he has called according to his purpose." Romans 8:28. All things work for the good for you just because you love God and you are called according to his purpose. Do not be discouraged when you face many difficulties, just know that all things are working out for your own good. Your struggles will produce perseverance and faith. It works out at the end.

GOD'S PURPOSE

CHAPTER ONE

DISCOVER GOD'S PURPOSE FOR YOUR LIFE

Purpose by definition is the reason for existence. It is the answer to the question, why? Why you were created, why you exist, why you are here on earth and why you do what you do? The purpose of a thing is usually defined by the one who created it. Nobody creates a product without clearly defining what it will be used for. Every created thing we see has a particular purpose it is serving. You were also created by God for a unique purpose that you are supposed to serve. You have a purpose here on earth; you were created with unique talents and gifts that you are supposed to manifest.

Dr Myles Munroe says, "The greatest tragedy of life is not death, it is living a life without a purpose." Not knowing why you exist is the greatest tragedy most people live with. Life is hard to get by if you really don't know why you exist. Most people tiptoe to their grave frustrated and unhappy because they don't know why they exist. If you want your life to have meaning and significance you should find and fulfil God's purpose for your life.

The truth of the matter we should all embrace is that God created all of us for a special purpose. Your purpose is unique to yourself; it is different from everyone else's. If you haven't discovered what your purpose is, you have an obligation to find out what it is. You need to search within and unearth the gifts and talents that God placed inside of you in order for you to fulfil the reason why you exist. You can only find meaning, develop and maximize your potential by finding the question to your why and pursuing it.

GOD CREATED YOU FOR A PURPOSE

Rick Warren said, "You were created by God on purpose for a purpose." God was intentional in creating you, and his intentions were for you to manifest your gifts to the world. He prepared your purpose even before you were conceived in your mother's womb. He said to Jeremiah, "Before I formed you in the womb I knew you, before you were born I set you apart; I appointed you as a prophet to the nation." Jeremiah 1:5. God knows everything and everyone even before conception and birth. He knows why he created you and he has set you apart to fulfil that purpose.

God spoke to Jeremiah about his intentions he had with him way before he was born at the time where Jeremiah was not confident by his call to be the prophet. Jeremiah's purpose of being a prophet was not an easy one. He was called to warn of the destruction and disaster to befall nations including Babylon, and confronting kings and other nations. It was a tough call indeed and Jeremiah was afraid to get heed of it. God has already given you a divine appointment no matter how tough it is. God created you for a purpose and he has set you apart to be an instrument of good works before your conception and birth.

God prepared you before birth ahead of your purpose that he created you for. The Apostle Paul also said that, "But when God, who set me apart from my mother's womb and called me by his grace, was pleased." Galatians 1:15. You are not a biological accident, God created you for a purpose. Your parents might not have planned to have you, but God had already planned and mapped the way for you. You have a purpose you need to carry despite your race, gender, social and economic status. You have the right ingredients to carry out God's purpose in your life.

God created you for a purpose. The scripture says, "For we are God's handiwork, created in Christ Jesus to do good works, which God prepared in advance for us to do." Ephesians 2:10. You are God's handiwork; you are his masterpiece and hand crafted by God himself. You were created for the purpose of doing the good works and he already prepared you in advance to carry out the same purpose. God created you for a purpose of doing the good work for the benefit of you and others.

From birth, God has been further preparing you ahead of your purpose. The experiences you go through – the positive and negative, your talents and capabilities you have are necessary for shaping and moulding you to become ready for your purpose. God had a design and plan all mapped out for you to make the work easier for you. He knows exactly what he wants you to accomplish. You don't think, talk, walk or do what you do by accident. It is by God's design. God created you for a purpose, unique to yourself. God created you and knows the plans for you. Let's now look at how you can discover your life purpose.

How to Discover God's Purpose

Purpose gives you reason to live. Without realizing your purpose you might struggle to find meaning, significance and passion. You will be aimlessly living your life because you don't have any idea of what it should be used for. Your life matters; God created you knowing the impact you should make with your life. It is of greater importance for you to discover and live your purpose. I am convinced that it should be every person's goal to discover their purpose and be what they were created to be. Discovering God's purpose for your life is an exciting journey which is worthwhile to embark on. Here are some the ways you can discover your purpose.

SPEND MORE TIME WITH GOD

The answer as to why you were created is found in the one who created you. He is the one who has the full manual of why you exist and how you function. God knows why he created you. God reviews everything through the Holy Spirit. One of the reasons why God created you is for you to have a good relationship with him. When you have a good relationship with the creator it becomes easy to know why he created you. You can only know his purpose and plan for your life if you spend more time with him. The same that you do with your relationships with your family, and friends, you can only get to understand them and their plans when you have a good relationship.

Cultivate a good relationship with God through reading the bible, spending more time in prayer and trusting him. The bibles says, "Trust in the LORD with all your heart and lean not on your own understanding; in all your ways submit to him, and he will make your paths straight." Proverbs 3:5-6. Every relationship is built on trust, when you trust the God with all your heart without leaning on your own understanding he will show you his purpose for your life.

You are God's creation, created by him for him. It is said in Colossians that "For in him all things were created: things in heaven and on earth, visible and invisible, whether thrones or powers or rulers or authorities; all things have been created through him and for him." Colossians 1:16. God created all things that we see and don't see the things on the earth and heaven for his own purpose. He created you for the advancement of his agenda, only God can show you that which he created you for.

KNOW YOUR GIFTS

You have unique natural talents and gifts that you were created with. Natural gifts are the abilities that you were born with. These talents are part of you and they are innate. Gifts include artistic skills, athletic skills, intelligence among other different skills people possess. These gifts are part of your ultimate purpose why you are here on earth. Some of the gifts you have might lie dormant in you without you realizing how gifted you. You need to search within yourself and know your God given talents that you should use for the good works he created you for.

The bible also speaks about the spiritual gifts which we all possess. Some are given gifts of the apostles, prophets, evangelist, pastors and teachers to equip his people for the work. "So Christ himself gave the apostles, the prophets, the evangelists, the pastors and teachers, to equip his people for works of service, so that the body of Christ may be built up until we all reach unity in the faith and in the knowledge of the Son of God and become mature, attaining to the whole measure of the fullness of Christ." Ephesians 4:11-16.

Apostle Paul in Romans also speaks about the spiritual gifts as gifts we received according to the grace we received and our faith in God, "We have different gifts, according to the grace given to each of us. If your gift is prophesying, then prophesy in accordance with your faith; if it is serving, then serve; if it is teaching, then teach; if it is to encourage, then give encouragement; if it is giving, then give generously; if it is to lead, do it diligently; if it is to show mercy, do it cheerfully." Romans 12:6-8. The purpose of these gifts is to equip you to carry out the purpose God created you for.

Gifts are like seeds which grow to bear fruit. These seeds only grow when you make use of them. Are you good with people, are you a good communicator, are you compassionate, are you good with administration, do you possess the spiritual gifts like that of apostle, prophets, evangelist and teachers? Surely there is an area that you are gifted in; those gifts are where your purpose lies. Use them for the purpose that you were created for.

God gave you talents which he expects you to use it. Jesus talks about the parable of the ten talents where the master gave ten talents to his three servants. The first servant worked ten more talents; the second one worked five more talents while the third and last servant kept his talent on the cloth and did nothing with it. His talent was taken away from him and given to his other two colleagues who put theirs to good use were rewarded. You are expected to work out and exercise your talents that God gave you.

FIND YOUR PASSION

God's purpose is also found in your passion. Passion is simply defined as an intense feeling towards something. It is that compelling desire and very intense enthusiasm that you develop towards something or someone. It could be a passion for a cause, idea or emotion towards someone or something. Passion finds you

11

doing things that are easy and with utmost fulfilment and joy. That very thing you are passionate about or love doing is an indicator of your life purpose. It gives you the energy and drive to pursue your purpose in life. Your passion will keep on going even when you are about to give up. Passion is the fuel that keeps the dream train moving forward.

Your passion is found in those things that you love doing. It can also be found in those things that annoy or give you a burden. Your passion points out where your purpose lies. To find your passion take note of those things that brings you utmost and genuine joy to you. Things like spending more time with people, giving to the less privileged, counselling others, caring for children, cooking, and gardening, among others. Passion is found in those daily mundane activities that you always do. They give you an idea of what your passion is.

Try to follow your own passion other than other people's passion. Sometimes in trying to please the people close to us like our friends, family and colleagues we tend to follow their interests, suggestions and passion forgetting your own. Robert Ballard once said that, "Follow your own passion—not your parents', not your teachers'—yours." It is good to draw inspiration from others but you should be careful to follow their passion and forget yours. The more you do what you love the more you find where your true passion is.

LOOK FOR WAYS YOU CAN POSITIVELY IMPACT OTHERS

Purpose can be found in what you can do for others with what you have where you are. Rather than focusing on what you need and makes you happy, you should also look at what others need and what makes them happy. The greatest purpose of human kind is service to others. You start living a purpose driven life when you start serving people other than yourself. There is definitely something that you can do to help and reach someone thereby making a positive impact in their lives.

Look for ways you can positively impact and contribute to your family, friends and the community you live in. Look for the people's needs which you can easily reach out to. Usually people's needs are wrapped in the challenges they face each day. Find ways you can positively contribute towards the betterment of their lives. You can make an impact by doing small gestures like helping someone blind cross the busy street, letting someone on the rush go before you in a grocery store, being kind to the needy on the street etc. The more you serve others the more you find fulfilment and joy, and more importantly finding your passion.

CHAPTER TWO

PURSUING
GOD'S PURPOSE

Discovering your purpose is only part of the process, pursuing it completes it. After you have discovered God's purpose for your life, you need to make a conscious decision and commitment to pursue it. There are those needles fears and small voices that you need to be careful about. Jeremiah also had those when he was called to pursue his purpose, "But the Lord said to me, "Do not say, 'I am too young.' You must go to everyone I send you to and say whatever I command you. Do not be afraid of them, for I am with you and will rescue you," declares the Lord." Jeremiah 1:7-8. God told Jeremiah to carry out his purpose as per God's instruction because God himself will be with him to rescue him.

You might feel that you are not good enough to be carrying out your God given purpose. You doubt yourself and your capabilities when you look at your background, level of education, age, gender and experience. Don't be afraid as God to Jeremiah, he shall be with you. He wouldn't give you the assignment if he knew you are not capable of accomplishing it. Have the courage to act on your purpose and here are some of ways to help you in pursuit of your purpose.

PUT GOD FIRST

Everything starts with having a good relationship with the one who has a purpose for you. Have a good relationship with God, prioritize his purpose for you and become what he created you to be. The only way you can pursue his purpose is by making him a priority in everything you do. I know with business of life, your pursuit of own priorities life family, friends, dreams, hobbies and careers; these things seek your attention. Your own priorities should not be the reason for you not to prioritize God's priorities to pursue his purpose.

When you put God first he will guide and direct you towards achieving his purpose. God will show you what you need to do in order to get where he wants you to go. God will provide all the necessary resources required for you to fulfil what he called you to do. He is the one that initiated the process and he knows better how you should go about it.

Put him first, even when you are not sure what to do and which way to take he will show you. God is systematic, he does things in a more organised and orderly manner. He wouldn't require of you what he hadn't already ordained you to do. Whatever you need to fulfil his purpose put him first.

After the death of Moses, Joshua took over the responsibility to lead the children of Israel to the Promised Land and God said to Joshua, "Keep this Book of the Law always on your lips; meditate on it day and night, so that you may be careful to do everything written in it. Then you will be prosperous and successful. Have I not commanded you? Be strong and courageous. Do not be afraid; do not be discouraged, for the Lord your God will be with you wherever you go." Joshua 1:8-9.

God tells Joshua to take heed of the word of God, meditating on it each time and doing everything that it says. He was also instructed not to be afraid for God himself will see to it that his purpose will be accomplished with him by his side. If God calls you to do something, he will see to it that it is fulfilled. He is always with you as you pursue his purpose. Put him first.

When you put God first, trusting and depending on his power your pursuit of purpose becomes easy. Through his word you will get wisdom, encouragement, strength and direction of what to do. Through the Holy Spirit you will get guidance on how you should do things. When you put God first he will give you all the strength, wisdom, courage and tenacity you need to pursue his purpose. Put God first and everything else will fall into place.

RELY UPON GOD'S WAYS

When you are pursuing your purpose you should rely on God's way. God's way is always the best way. He has everything figured out even before you get to know about it. God had already figured out your purpose and planned everything for you before you were even conceived by your parents. It is said about God's ways in Isaiah that, "For my thoughts are not your thoughts, neither are your ways my ways, declares the Lord. As the heavens are higher than the earth, so are my ways higher than your ways and my thoughts than your thoughts." Isaiah 55:8-9.

God has every account of everything about us and that we will ever do. When we rely upon his ways even when things get out of hand, you will need strength to keep going forward. Apostle Paul said, "Do not be anxious about anything, but in every situation, with prayer and petition, with thanksgiving, present your requests to God." Philippians 4:6. In every situation make your request known to God through prayer, petition and thanksgiving. Isaiah also says that, "But those who wait on the LORD will renew their strength. They will soar on wings like eagles; they will run and not grow weary, they will walk and not faint." Isaiah 40:31. Relying on God makes your pursuit of purpose an easy go even when things gets tough and you feel like giving up, He will renew your strength.

PRAY CONSISTENTLY

When you pursue God's purpose you must be consistently in prayer. God answers prayers and whenever you seek his will and guidance in pursuing his purpose just pray. God is the one who began the work in you and praying to him about it is collaborating with him in fulfilling his purpose. You need to consistently, earnestly and fervently pray to God about your purpose. Apostle Paul said that, "Don't worry about anything, but pray and ask God for everything you need, always giving thanks for what you have." Philippians 4:6. Always pray for what you need God to do.

Jesus Christ himself was consistently praying and most remarkable people in the bible consistently prayed. Moses prayed for God to be with him ahead of his purpose of delivering the children of Israel and God assured him that he was going to be with him when he parted the red sea. David prayed and God gave him strength, Solomon prayed and he was given wisdom. Daniel also prayed consistently before the Lord three times a day and God delivered him. Apostle Paul prayed consistently pleading with the Lord to take his pain away and God reassured him that his grace is sufficient and God's strength was made perfect in weakness.

Prayer is very important as you pursue your purpose because it connects you and help you create a close relationship with God. Through him you are revitalised and strengthened just like what David did, you will gain understanding of the will of God over your life and purpose. Through prayer you get the assurance of the Lord as you pursue your purpose. Prayer is the only weapon you need to overcome any challenges you will face as you pursue your purpose. Constantly pray and you will effectively pursue your purpose.

BELIEVE IN THE PROMISE OF GOD

Pursuing your purpose requires you to believe and have unwavering faith in God's promises. Fulfilling God's purpose on your own, leaning on your own understanding, abilities and strength will make your pursuit difficult. You need to have faith in him who started the good work in you for it is faithful to see you through the journey. For you to successfully pursue and fulfil your purpose you need a good relationship with God. Just like any other relationship, you can only have a good relationship with God if you believe and trust in his word and promises.

God is pleased by your faith. "And without faith it is impossible to please God, because anyone who comes to him must believe that he exists and that he rewards those who earnestly seek him." Hebrews 11:6. As you pursue your purpose come to God in faith believing in his promise that he exists and he will reward you for your earnest pursuit. Faith unlocks the doors for you and it helps you overcome any challenge that you will face along the way.

Faith attracts the power of the object of your faith. When you have faith in God (the object) you (the subject) submit yourself to the power of the one you believe. In other words you heavily rely on his power to face each difficulty you may encounter. Having faith attracts good things to you because you always gravitate towards through your belief. Believe in God's promises and you will rely on his power to have your purpose fulfilled.

Faith directs you towards the path that you should go. As you believe in God and his promises you solely depend on him and whenever you face any challenge God will show you the way to go. Strength is found in God through faith. It is said that battles are won and lost in the mind, when you have strong and unwavering faith you develop a strong and positive mind set which is a necessary condition for you to achieve your purpose. Faith is the oil needed to smoothen the journey of your pursuit of purpose.

BE STRONG AND COURAGEOUS

It takes courage to go after your dreams and pursue your purpose. Along the journey you may face difficulties, resistance and different challenges. You need courage, commitment and resilience to be able to face every challenge which comes your way. Without courage and strength you might easily give up on your pursuit of purpose. Be strong and courageous confidently knowing that God is with you until the completion of your work. "Being confident of this, that he who began a good work in you will carry it on to completion until the day of Christ Jesus." Philippians 1:6.

Joshua after assuming the responsibilities of Moses following his death, God told him to be strong and courageous because God was going to be with him. "Be strong and very courageous. Be careful to obey all the law my servant Moses gave you; do not turn from it to the right or to the left, that you may be successful wherever you go." Joshua 1:7. God understood that the task that was before Joshua was a great one indeed, taking the children of Israel to the promise land. So many challenges were faced along the way but Joshua was strong and courageous as instructed by God who had started the work with him.

It is written that, "So do not throw away your confidence; it will be richly rewarded. You need to persevere so that when you have done the will of God, you will receive what he has promised." Hebrews 10:35-36. Stay strong and courageous, don't throw your confidence away a great reward awaits after you are done with the way of God for your life. Things will be tough sometimes, you will face some difficulties every now and then but never give up, stay strong with your eyes fixed on the prize.

DON'T BE AFRAID TO FAIL

As you pursue your purpose things will not always be smooth. There will be times when you fail. You will not get it right the first time you start pursuing your purpose. Don't be afraid to fail, in fact fail big. Failure and success are synonyms you can't really have one without the other. Failure is part of the success process. When you fail, try again and again until you get it right. Failure is not the roadblock to you realizing your purpose it is a detour which redirect you towards success.

Failure is inevitable especially when you are pursuing something of significance. Consistence and persistence are good twins you need to keep close in your chest in order to effectively deal with failure. Every failed attempt is a step closer to achieve your purpose that is if you are willing to learn, unlearn and relearn. Failure is a great opportunity for you to learn how to strategize and realign your goals and your purpose. Most people who pursued their dreams and lived their purpose never got it right the first time. But they took failure as a learning process rather than the end of the process.

GOD'S PURPOSE

CHAPTER THREE

IMPORTANCE OF
GOD'S PURPOSE

Seeking and pursuing God's purpose is very important. Having a purpose is the beginning of living a meaningful life. Purpose is the fuel that steers you towards achieving success and fulfilment. Living a purposeful life isn't just good for you, but for those around you as well your friends, family, and community. Those individuals who pursue their God given purpose have a positive effect on others. Purpose gives you the reason to live and you will find it exciting along the journey of life when you live your passion.

Most successful people have a common trait of living their lives on purpose. Purpose is the impetus that has a pulling force, pulling you towards becoming better and achieving your goals. Your purpose keeps the fire burning inside of you that leads you to do something significant with your life. Life lived on purpose is very meaningful and that on its own is enough for you to be able to leave a mark on this earth. Your existence adds value to other people's lives and yours too when you live a purposeful life. Life is more simplified when you know what you want, how you can get it and how you will use it. Planning becomes very easy for you and you can have clear defined goals and knowing where you are headed. Needless to say, living a purpose driven life is very important and here are some of the reasons why.

YOU LIVE A MEANINGFUL LIFE

You don't exist here on earth for the sake of just existing, you are here on a special purpose and that purpose gives your life meaning. A meaningful life is the life you find fulfilling and satisfying especially when you feel that there is a link between your biological existence and the relative meaning for your existence. Everyone has a need to feel significant and have relevance in life. When you live a purpose driven life, you satisfy that need by having a meaningful life. With purpose life becomes meaningful and have clear direction when life is meaningful it becomes fulfilling and satisfying.

In his book Man's Search for Meaning Viktor Frankl said that, "A man who becomes conscious of the responsibility he bears toward a human being who affectionately waits for him, or to an unfinished work, will never be able to throw away his life. He knows the "why" for his existence, and will be able to bear almost any "how"." When you live a meaningful life, you will never waste your life for anything and you can bear with almost everything that comes your way. A meaningful life gives you a reason to be alive each day.

When you live a meaningful life you don't hang around toxic and negative people who don't seem to aspire to do anything with their lives. With a purposeful and meaningful life you don't waste your time and energy doing unfulfilling tasks and work you will always do the things that bring value both to you and others. You don't just randomly live when you live a fulfilled life.

PASSION AND DRIVE

Success requires a relentless passion and drive to get things done. It is easy to have a burning passion and a constant drive when doing the things you are designed to do. Living your life on purpose stirs the passion and drive within you to make great accomplishments. With passion and drive it is difficult to give up or give in on your purpose no matter how bad the situation gets. Passion drives hard work, and strong determination to get things done.

All successful people who made an impact on others while pursuing their purpose had an intriguing passion and drive towards whatever they were doing. With passion you will be creative in solving challenges and not giving up. With passion and drive you will be motivated to work hard and give whatever it takes even when you are not sure how. Passion helps you in accomplishing your goals and dreams.

With passion and drive, pursuing God's purpose becomes part of you rather than an obligation. You develop a stronger desire to do what you are supposed to do beyond just doing it for duty. With passion you will be effective in making a positive impact on others. You will be relentless, and ambitious to do the best with what you have to make the best out of every situation. Passion is the fuel that makes your purpose possible.

YOU EXPERIENCE FULFILMENT AND SUCCESS

God's purpose for your life brings fulfilment and success. Purpose is the reason for existence and why you were created. Any product you see whether natural or man made is successful when it accomplishes what it was created to do. If a car is not transporting people and goods from one point to another it will not be fulfilling its purpose. The success of it as a product will not be achieved when it's stationery but when it's moving. God also created you for a purpose, your success and fulfilment comes from doing what you were created to accomplish. You will not find fulfilment and success when you are not doing your purpose.

Everyone has a need to be fulfilled and failure to feel fulfilled is a major cause for a miserable life. When you are not fulfilled by a job you will not find it satisfying and worth giving it your best. Chances are that job will be a source of your misery and other stress related conditions like high blood pressure. Some move from job to job just trying to find that job that makes them happy. When you live your life on purpose you will find fulfilment and success becomes inevitable.

You were created for a purpose, when you pursue that purpose life becomes satisfying. God created you to have a good relationship with him, worship him and use those gifts within you for the betterment of others. When you pursue your purpose fulfilment is guaranteed. You have a purpose higher than yourself, you have something to give. If you want to find fulfilment and success you must pursue your purpose.

When you find fulfilment and success you begin to live a life that is meaningful and impactful. You will find life worth living with a great satisfaction, improved self-esteem and great health. You begin to live a value based life where you will solve people's problems. You will find doing what you were created to do easy thereby positively impacting others. It becomes easy to pull others with you as you find life fulfilling and more meaningful.

YOU GET A SENSE OF DIRECTION AND FOCUS

God's purpose is a sure way to have a sense of direction and focus for your life. With the sense of direction and focus you can easily focus your time, resources and efforts towards achieving your purpose. Sense of direction sets you in motion towards making an impact in other people's lives and more focused on doing the things that matter.

Sense of direction and focus makes possible things which otherwise seemed difficult to accomplish. When you have a purpose that you are constantly and persistently pursuing each time, accomplishing that purpose becomes possible. With focus and direction you seize every opportunity that comes your way. You will use time effectively knowing what needs to be done and when.

CHAPTER FOUR

OVERCOMING
THE OBSTACLES

When pursuing your purpose challenges and obstacles are inevitable. Challenges are part of growth and the success process. Many great individuals who did outstanding and great things faced different challenges along the way. They prevailed against the hardships and diverse challenges. Many people stop their pursuit of their purpose when faced with different challenges. You don't really fail when you're faced with challenges; you only fail when you allow the challenges to stop you from pursuing your purpose.

The real test is not in the challenges; it is in not giving up in the midst of all the challenges. Obstacles are just detours that you face in this journey of pursuing your purpose. Challenges are also necessary to strengthen you, they are valuable learning processes and they facilitate growth. Every challenging moment builds your character and your attitude which is necessary for your success. Here are some of the challenges that stop people from pursuing their purpose.

OBSTACLES FACED WHEN PURSUING YOUR PURPOSE

FEAR

Everything in life has a degree of uncertainty; this uncertainty causes fear. Fear is such a very powerful force. Fear affects the decisions you will make and your decisions affect the outcomes. Fear may prevent you from doing something that is not good for you, however if not managed well, fear can have you stuck and hold you back from realizing the potential to fulfil your purpose. For you to fulfil you purpose, you need to leverage on your fears.

People have different fears that drive them. Some have a fear of failure, fear of rejection and fear of success. These fears can literally kill your dreams and stop you from pursuing your purpose. Fear keeps you stuck in your comfort zone and unable to do anything more with your life. Fear legitimizes all the reasons good enough to hold you back from pursuing your purpose. Fear is another sure way to keep procrastinating.

The fear of failure is the cognitive and emotional reaction to the perceived consequences of failure to achieve your purpose. Sometime you stop doing what you are supposed to do not because you have failed but because you are afraid to fail. Moses was afraid to pursue his mission because he thought to himself that he was going to fail to convince people that he was sent by God.

Knowing the people whom he was going to deliver very well, fear of failure grappled with him so much that he ended up giving God a lot of excuses not to go back to Egypt.

With the fear of failure you will be worried about what will people say if you fail which will result in your reluctance to act. Fear of failure causes you to have emotional and physical challenges like fatigue and becoming emotionally drained. Fear of failure robs you of the pleasure found in pursuing your purpose and dreams. It causes you to be stuck in hopelessness and chronic worry.

Everyone wants people to accept them and like them. When pursuing your dreams seem to threaten that need for acceptance it causes fear of rejection. Fear of rejection has stopped many people from doing what they were supposed to do. It could be rejection from a university, job and people you love. Moses being a fugitive who ran from Egypt for him to go back to the same place he ran away from for reasons known by everyone he was afraid people would reject him.

Fear of rejection causes people to do things that they would not otherwise do or that is not in line with their purpose just for the sake of being accepted. Fear of rejection might be caused by how you think people think of you in view of your purpose. Sometimes when people know of you for something else, it is hard for them to accept you for what you want to do or change in you. When your purpose calls you do what your friends and family are not doing, you may feel that they will reject you because of that. Fear of rejection keeps you from making steps towards your purpose.

As funny as it may sound, some people don't pursue their purpose because of fear of success. Yes, is there a thing such as this you may wonder? If you are afraid of success you may find yourself not doing the things you have to do to realize your potential. Success is scary for many; it brings with it many changes. It brings increased responsibilities, expectations and carries within itself change of habits and behavior. Many are afraid that things may probably work out and they find themselves stuck in indecision.

SELF-DOUBT

Self-doubt is when you feel that you are not capable or the right person to be doing that which you are supposed to do. It is when you lack self-confidence with yourself, your skills and competence to do something. Self-doubt keeps you from pursuing your life purpose. With self-doubt the fear of failure grows too quickly and withers your potential to pursue your purpose. Self-doubt causes you to fail before even starting because you would have disqualified yourself already.

Self-doubt can be caused by your upbringing and background. Your background plays a very pivotal role in developing confidence in yourself. Your upbringing has impact on how you think and react to situations. If you were brought up in a toxic environment where you were constantly told that you will not amount to anything it may affect the way you look at yourself. It can stop you from pursuing your purpose thinking that you are not good enough. This has an ultimate effect on your self-confidence in pursuing your purpose.

Past mistakes and experiences affect your perception about yourself. The mistakes you made and the experiences you went through can make you see yourself as unworthy to do anything meaningful. If you experienced negative situations growing up like bad family relationships, physical and emotional abuse it affects the way you see yourself. You might have made a mistake like Moses who murdered an Egyptian, Paul persecuted the followers of Jesus and David committed murder and adultery. Mistakes can make you disqualify yourself of pursuing your purpose if you allow them to make you feel unworthy.

Self-doubt is sometimes a result of comparison with other people. Sometimes it comes natural to compare ourselves with family members, friends and colleagues. There is nothing wrong with that, it can help you push your limits to become better and also learn from them too. However, when the comparison becomes the barometer to your self-confidence it keeps you from achieving your purpose. Someone will always be smarter and ahead of you in a way, if you allow that to make you have self-doubt you will become an obstacle to your own success.

When you don't know what to do when a challenge comes

your way it can leave you having self-doubt. It is a given that, when you are pursuing your purpose you will face some difficulties and failure to deal with those difficulties may leave you feeling that you are not worth it. If you don't have any experience in dealing with such challenges you might be clouded with feelings of insecurity and uncertainty. This will make you feel like you are not worth pursuing your goals.

Fear of failure causes people to have self-doubt. Everyone wants to get it right the first time they do anything. The feeling of perfection in doing things can stop you from even trying out something. Whenever you feel that you might not get it right or fail you may end up feeling that you can't do it. If you are looking for perfection all the time it will stop you from acting in order to save yourself from the disappointment of failing.

UNBELIEF

Unbelief can paralyze your ability to fulfil your purpose. Unbelief is when you lack trust and confidence in someone or something. Unbelief or lack of trust or faith in God keeps you from successfully pursuing God's purpose for your life. It is the stop sign for many to be able to accomplish what is necessary for them to accomplish their purpose. Unbelief makes it hard for God to help you through your purpose if you don't believe in him.

Jesus had an account where people had unbelief about him. "Coming to his hometown, he began teaching the people in their synagogue, and they were amazed. "Where did this man get this wisdom and these miraculous powers?" they asked. "Isn't this the carpenter's son? Isn't his mother's name Mary, and aren't his brothers James, Joseph, Simon and Judas? Aren't all his sisters with us? Where then did this man get all these things?" And they took offense with him. But Jesus said to them, "A prophet is not without honour except in his own town and in his own home." And he did not do many miracles there because of their lack of faith." Matthew 13:58.

The lack of conviction of their purpose causes people to have unbelief. Many people in Jesus's hometown assumed that they knew Jesus very well and they were not convinced about his purpose here on earth. Just because they knew him and his family they were not really convinced that he could be the messiah. Many people today lack the conviction that God can do something with their lives maybe because of their backgrounds or upbringing. The lack of conviction ultimately makes people act in disbelief if they really have a purpose to fulfil.

The ignorance of God's promises and word also cause many to wail in unbelief. Many people act out of ignorance of the word of God and its promises. Hosea writes that, "My people are destroyed from lack of knowledge. "Because you have rejected knowledge, I also reject you as my priests; because you have ignored the law of your God, I also will ignore your children." Hosea 4:6. God says people suffer and are being destroyed because they lack knowledge. Ignorance destroys people's potential to realize their purpose in life.

GIVING UP TOO EASILY

Pursuing your purpose requires determination and unwavering resilience. One of the challenges most people face is giving up too easily on their purpose. Most people need to see the results and success instantly; they give up when that don't happen. Every great person has faced so many challenges and they succeeded not because they avoided the challenges by giving up so easily. That is what separates those who fail from those who succeed in pursuing the purpose.

Most people give up too easily and too early because someone told them that they can't do it. People who don't understand what you do and why you are doing it there is a tendency to discourage you from doing it. Some will actually discourage you from doing something based on their own lack of ability to do it. They will tell you that you can't do something just because they can't do it themselves and you give up too early.

When you too comfortable with the way things are you are likely to give up too early on pursuing a purpose that stretches and challenges your status quo. Feeling too comfortable with your current status quo causes a lot of people to back down when they face challenges after pursuing their purpose. Always feeling that you have a fall-back position causes you not to focus your energy and resources towards achieving your purpose.

Distractions cause some people to easily give up on their purpose. Pursuing your purpose requires focus, discipline and consistent. Without these pursuing your purpose becomes challenging. Too many distractions from other aspects not related to other than your purpose can distract you from being attentive and focusing on your purpose. The distractions could be people and other actives that keep you from pursuing your purpose.

LACK OF DIRECTION AND FOCUS

Sense of direction and focus makes possible things which otherwise seemed difficult to accomplish. The lack of sense of direction and focus affect the progress you make in pursuing your purpose or anything in life. It is a challenge you may face when you have to many distractions and you are not too sure of your purpose. Sometimes with paralysis analysis which causes information overload being focused to make the right decision might be problematic.

OVERCOMING THE OBSTACLES

CONQUER FEAR

Fear, if not managed well can be the reason for you to give up on your purpose and dreams. You need to conquer all your fears and leverage on them to succeed on your purpose. Fear is not real after all; it is only false evidence appearing real. If you allow it to have permanence in your life you will not realize your purpose. Fear causes you to be reluctant to try out or do what is necessary for you to realize your purpose. It is the main reason why many people self-sabotage themselves resulting in them procrastinating, being anxious and stressed. Fear is the enemy of progress. Here are some of the ways you can conquer your fears.

TAKE SMALL STEPS

Fear comes in different forms and sizes. If you find yourself faced with seemingly overwhelming tasks to be accomplished in order to fulfil your purpose, the fear of failure immediately grapples them and they get stuck in indecision. Big goals require big steps and those big steps require confidence and great courage. If you are afraid of taking the big steps start small.

Break down all the things to be accomplished it small day by day, week by week and month by month goals that you can follow through without much anxiety and stress. Take a step at a time towards achieving your purpose. Instead of being worried about the ultimate big goal that you want to achieve you focus on the journey that you are taking towards achieving that big goal.

Taking small steps and focusing on a goal at a time is not only helpful in dealing with your fears but the more you achieve each goal the closer you get to realize your goals. The small steps help you move out of your comfort zone where fears keeps you stuck in.

LEARN FROM FAILURE

When the fear of failure stops you from pursuing your goals, you are short changing yourself of the valuable lessons that are learned from failure. There are more incredible and valuable lessons that you can learn from failure. Failure is not final; you only fail if you allow it to stop you from pursuing your purpose. Henry Ford said something interesting about failure, "Failure is simply the opportunity to begin again, this time more intelligently." Failing is simply an opportunity to try again, with intelligence learned from the previous failed attempt.

Failure on its own teaches you valuable lessons that are necessary for you to succeed. In fact failure is a prerequisite for success. With failure you learn to be resilient, courageous, flexible, adaptive and most important it changes your attitude towards success and life in general. All these things are necessary for you to succeed in pursuing your dreams. Don't be afraid to fail rather be willing to learn when you fail. Failure redirects and realigns you to your purpose.

YOU NEED TO LET GO

When your status quo is challenge there is a fear of unknown that holds you back from doing things that are different from the familiar. You keep holding on to the things that you are used to and feel they empower and give you comfort. These things we seem to hold on to usually hold you down and keep you from pursuing your purpose. It could be loved ones and close friends who sometimes hold you down from pursuing your purpose.

Once you accept that you can't do something because of someone else reasons you will stop pursuing your dreams. The fears themselves that you feel need to be let go. Let go of anything that fuels the fears in you. Focus more on the objectives than what you are afraid of. Go after your purpose and let go of your fears.

FACE THE FEAR WITH CONFIDENCE

There are many instances in the Bible where individuals called to fulfil God's purpose were filled with fear. Moses and Jeremiah are notable example who faced great fears but God reassured them that he was going to be with them through the journey. You need to face the fear with confidence that God will not leave you nor forsake you. He shall be with you while you realize your purpose of what you were created for.

It is written that, "The Lord himself goes before you and will be with you; he will never leave you nor forsake you. Do not be afraid; do not be discouraged." Deuteronomy 13:8. Whenever you are faced with fear or any difficulty just know that God will always be with you and before you. You can always rely on his strength and power because he promised never to leave you or forsake you. Never let fear discourage you into giving up, have confidence in what God promises.

You might be afraid of pursuing God's purpose for your life because of fear of failure and rejection. Even when success doesn't seem immediate or possible just know that all things work to your advantage. "And we know that in all things God works for the good of those who love him, who have been called according to his purpose." Romans 8:28. Even when you make mistakes just know that all things works for the good to those who are called according to his purpose. Overcome the fear with confidence that all things are working for your good.

We were created by God for his purpose on purpose. He is the one who called you out to fulfil his purpose and he is going to see it through so don't be afraid. "But now, this is what the Lord says— he who created you, Jacob, he who formed you, Israel: "Do not fear, for I have redeemed you; I have summoned you by name; you are mine." Isaiah 43:1. God calls us to have no fear and not to worry about how you are going to fulfil your purpose.

BELIEVE IN YOURSELF

The feeling of self-doubt can leave you feeling like you are not worth anything significant in your life. Self-doubt destroys your potential to pursue your purpose. It is a sure way of sabotaging yourself in pursuant of your dreams. Self-doubt is an obstacle that you face in realizing your dreams. In order to overcome this obstacle, you need to believe in yourself.

BE POSITIVE ABOUT YOURSELF

Believing in yourself means believing in your abilities. For you to believe in yourself requires you to have a positive outlook about yourself. Your success in pursuing your dreams has nothing to do with your upbringing or background. Never feel discouraged by what happened to you in the past you should focus on the future. Be positive about yourself, it is necessary for you to realize your purpose.

If you are constantly filling yourself with negativity, always filling your mind with negative self-talk you will develop negative attitude towards yourself. When you are negative it hard for you to get positive results. Negative self-talk will have some damaging consequences like stress, anxiety and depression. These will stop you from becoming effective in realizing your full potential.

You need to constantly be thinking and having positive self-talk. With positive thinking you create positive energy and stimulus to achieving your purpose. Being positive brings a lot of constructive changes that are necessary to pursuing your purpose and dreams. Positivity changes your attitude which is prerequisite to your success. With the right attitude you can surely achieve anything. Positive attitude affects your drive as it causes you to be more optimistic about purpose.

When you are positive about yourself you don't easily give up on your purpose. You stay committed and dedicated to your purpose until you fulfil it. As you stay committed in pursuing your goals you will begin to realize some abilities that you have and become aware of untapped potential within you to do something great. Positive thinking bridges the gap between success and failure.

Positive thinking causes you to be more focused on the goal. It gives you the sense of direction and effectively planning towards achieving your purpose. You don't give up in the face of any difficulties that you may encounter when you think positive about yourself. You have what it take to realize your purpose and impact others and it will take persistence to realize that purpose. Positive thinking is the fuel you need for you to be persistently pushing for your dreams.

When you think positively about yourself you begin to have more confidence in yourself. When you are confident about yourself you get to make the right choices that aid fulfilment of your purpose. You plan and execute your plans effortlessly which is necessary for realizing your purpose. Even when fear cloud your mind use positive thinking to overcome the obstacle by thinking of better ways to accomplish those goals.

VISUALISE YOUR SUCCESS

Visualizing your success that you want to see is very necessary for you to believe in yourself. All the top performers in different disciplines see themselves being at the top first before they actually accomplish it. When you are pursuing your purpose see yourself as if you have already succeeded. See yourself as if you have already won and victory becomes certain. Visualize your success each minute of the day, do the things that makes that image become a reality and success is inevitable.

Visualizing your success before you attain it gives you the determination to work towards your dreams. Picture yourself victorious as if you have already arrived where you are supposed to go. Picture yourself beyond all the challenges and circumstances that you might be facing. Forget about the past and current mistakes that you made and focus on the picture that you are visualizing in your mind. The more you picture yourself as victorious the more you conquer the obstacle of self-doubt and believe more in yourself.

REINFORCE YOUR PAST SUCCESS

If you want to believe in yourself you need to reinforce your past successes. You need to be constantly thinking about what you managed to achieve before so that you get the confidence that you can still do more. When you have self-doubt and not believing in yourself you begin to feel down and lose hope. You stop believing in what you are doing and that it is possible and can actually be successful. You need to remind yourself of how well you did in the past. Remind yourself of the success you achieved before.

Not believing yourself is the most self-inflicted disease that can stop you from living your purpose. Have faith in yourself by feeling proud of what you are able to accomplish. The best way to do that is by reinforcing the fact that you did it once then you can still do it. The more you reinforce your success in your subconscious mind, you will reinforce positivity and faith that is necessary for you to pursue your purpose.

BE CAREFUL OF THE NAYSAYERS

Sometimes you doubt yourself not because of your inability to do something but because somebody made you believe that you can't be successful. If you constantly find yourself listening to what people tell you about yourself you are highly likely to be what they think you are. Be careful of what you listen to and what people say about you and your ability to accomplish your purpose.

Some people will talk you down and out of your purpose. They will tell you that you are not good enough and smart enough to fulfil your purpose. Noah faced the same challenge when he invited people to help him build the ark which God had instructed him to build. A lot of folk tried to talk him out of his purpose and many discouraged him about pursuing his purpose but he never gave up.

If you listen to people tell you about what they think is possible for you and believe them you will have given them the power to direct your life. Sometimes when the naysayers say what they say and you start comparing yourself with other people pursuing their purpose you might end up having self-doubt about your own purpose. Just because you are doing something different from others doesn't mean that you can't do it. Stop listening to naysayers and focus on fulfilling your purpose just as Noah did with his purpose of building the ark.

SURROUND YOURSELF WITH THE RIGHT PEOPLE

When you get rid of the naysayers, you need to surround yourself with the right people. Those who can encourage, teach, direct and guide you to pursue your life purpose. You need the people who can water you and are keen to help you become what you were created to be. They could be family, friends, church members and mentors, it is very important to have them by your side as you pursue your purpose.

It is said that if you want to go faster go alone, but if you want to go further go with others. If you surround yourself with positive thinking people with the positive energy you will find yourself moving further towards your dreams. You are better off when you find someone who has walked down the path you are walking in order to help and guide you. These people are mentors; they help you realize your purpose by teaching you through the process to get there. Surround yourself with the right people who can help you go further in your purpose that way you will have confidence in yourself.

HAVE FAITH IN GOD

Having faith in God and believing in his promises is a sure way to overcome the unbelief obstacles to pursue your purpose. God created you for a purpose and in order for you to successfully pursue and fulfil that purpose you need to have unwavering faith in him. You need to have faith in him and believing his promises that he will see you through your purpose.

STUDY THE WILL OF GOD

You need to study the will of God for you to have faith in him. You need to know more about God and his will for you to develop the faith necessary for you to realize your purpose. "Consequently, faith comes from hearing the message, and the message is heard through the word of Christ." Romans 10:17.

If you are ignorant about the will of God and his promises you will undoubtedly have unbelief. Unbelief will stop you from accessing the necessary tools you need to pursue your purpose which is faith. Ignorance is a weapon the devil takes advantage of to get you way from realizing your purpose. You need to study the word of God in order to know your purpose and his promises. Knowing the will of God gives you the direction you need to pursue your purpose.

BELIEVE IN THE WORD OF GOD

When you study the word of God believe in it. Believe in what it says about your purpose. As you believe in the word of God you will overcome any doubt that you may have about your purpose. When the father who was possessed by the unclean spirit came to Jesus he told him to believe all things are possible. "If you can'?"

said Jesus. "Everything is possible for one who believes." Immediately the boy's father exclaimed, "I do believe; help me overcome my unbelief!" Mark 9:23-24.

The Bible tells us that we all have received a measure of faith that was distributed by God. "For by the grace given me I say to every one of you: Do not think of yourself more highly than you ought, but rather think of yourself with sober judgment, in accordance with the faith God has distributed to each of you." Romans 12:3. Jesus speaks about the power of faith and how much it can affect things. "He replied, "Because you have so little faith. Truly I tell you, if you have faith as small as a mustard seed, you can say to this mountain, 'Move from here to there,' and it will move. Nothing will be impossible for you." Matthew 17:20.

If you have faith in God nothing is too hard to do or accomplish. When you believe in what the word says, you shall see the glory of God. All things are possible if you believe in his word. Your purpose becomes possible if you have faith in his word. "Take away the stone," he said. "But, Lord," said Martha, the sister of the dead man, "by this time there is a bad odor, for he has been there four days." "Then Jesus said, "Did I not tell you that if you believe, you will see the glory of God?" John 11:39-40.

ACT UPON THE WORD OF GOD

The word of God tells us that we have a measure of faith distributed to each and every one of us. It is also stated on different accounts that if you believe you can do the impossible. The challenge is not in believing but in acting upon the word of God. Acting on the word of God completes everything. Your faith pleases God more than anything else. "And without faith it is impossible to please God, because anyone who comes to him must believe that he exists and that he rewards those who earnestly seek him." Hebrews 11:6.

In order to deal with unbelief you must act on the word of God, doing what it says you should. Faith without action is dead as the bible states it. "... Do you want evidence that faith without deeds is useless[a]?" James 2:20. When you have faith in God, you will produce good works and those good works will help in overcoming your unbelief. Put your faith into action and your faith can help others, "When Jesus saw their faith, he said to the paralyzed man, "Son, your sins are forgiven." Mark 2:5.

PRAY IN FAITH

Unbelief robs God on his ability to do great things. God can do anything he so wishes to do with your life but you can limit his ability to do so because of unbelief. Praying in faith can help you overcome the unbelief. When you pray earnestly to God you will be communicating with God through Jesus Christ and as you pray you create a good relationship with God. When you have a good relationship with God your faith becomes strong.

Let your life be a life of consistent and expectant prayers. By praying and submitting to God you allow him to do the work within you and helping you to overcome any doubt within. If there is anything that you know keeps you from believing God pray that you may repent from it so that there is nothing that hinders your faith in God. Every time when Jesus performed miracles he was marvelled by the faith people had, pray that you may also overcome your unbelief so that he can use you fully for his purpose.

NEVER GIVE UP

Giving up does not just stop you from achieving your purpose but it stops you from having the pleasure of doing things. It robs you of the pleasure found from trying. You need determination and unwavering resilience as you pursue your purpose. You will face some challenges but remember it always the darkest before dawn. The night might be too long but be rest assured that joy always comes in the morning. You might not get instant success results, you may face resistance, but that should not deter you from doing all you can in order to achieve your purpose.

Every person who was successful in pursuing their purpose never gave up. They were determined and focused to get things done no matter the circumstances. Giving up is the thin line that separates those who succeed in fulfilling their purpose from those who fail. You might have a thousand reasons for you to throw in the towel but I dare you to never give up in pursuing your purpose. You will find more fulfilment and success in pushing through than giving up.

Every time you feel like giving up remind yourself why you even started at the first place. Make your purpose the center of everything that you do. It is very easy to have the bigger picture as you pursue your purpose. Always think of why you are doing it, how it will impact others and how you will feel after achieving it. Think more about the results of the process instead of focusing on the difficulties of the process. The more you think about the ultimate goal to be achieved the more likely you are to overcome every challenge you will face along the way.

You need to have realistic expectations. Giving up too easily is sometimes caused by the frustration felt when you don't get the results you expected to get. If your experience doesn't meet your expectation you simply give up. You need realistic expectations that give you room to make mistakes and not perfectionism. Things might not work out the first time but embrace that and keep trying again. The more you are realistic in your expectations the less likely you are going to give up.

When you face rock bottom be willing to reroute yourself and get back on your feet. Mistakes are bound to happen and failure is inevitable but they should not be the reason why you give up on your purpose. Take every mistake and failure as a learning opportunity for you to become and do better next time. You need to be honest with yourself, admit where you were wrong and correct it for you to succeed. Failure should not be the reason for you to give up rather it should be the reason for you to keep trying because every failed attempt is a step closer to achieving your purpose.

Instead of giving up when you are faced with challenges, look back and celebrate all the successes you had. God has brought you thus far for a reason. There are successes that you had that you know God helped you with and victories he won for you. Be happy with what you have managed to accomplish so far. All the steps you have managed to take to get where you are and the obstacles that you have already overcome. Be grateful for all the trials and tribulations and know that God is in the midst.

Pursuing your purpose could be a tough journey with so many stumbling blocks along the way. One sure thing that can stop you from pursuing your purpose is accepting your hopelessness. When you tell yourself that there is nothing you can do over your situation sure enough there is absolutely nothing that you will be able to do or accomplish. You need to believe in yourself and refuse to be stuck in hopelessness. There is always something that you can do. You should always be solution conscious rather than be conscious. The more you look for solutions the more you have more hope in yourself. You need to have that leap of faith that what you are doing will work out for you.

Failure is not final but giving up completes it. No matter how many times you fail you should never give up. Keep trying until you find the solution to the challenges you are facing. You need to be constantly unlearning and relearning the ways to get back up and pursue your purpose. Perseverance and persistence is a sure way for you to achieve your purpose. Keep trying over and over again with faith that you will get it right this time. Never give up on God because he will never think above giving up on you. Keep the faith, keep trying and never give up until you fulfil your purpose.

STAY FOCUSED

A strong sense of determination and focus will help you achieve your purpose. To get started on your purpose is hard but staying focused is even harder. Sometimes you will start off highly motivated and highly determined to go after it until you get stuck on some challenges. Sometimes the frustration of failure, pressure of the work overload and distraction keep you from staying focused on your purpose. Sometimes with so much going on in your life you are easily derailed from pursuing your purpose and eventually give up. If you are going to successfully fulfil your life purpose you need to stay focused.

For you to stay focused you need to focus much on those things and processes that you can control and not really the outcomes.

When you get stuck at focusing on the outcomes it is easy to get overwhelmed and lose focus on what you want. Do what you can with what you have at that particular moment and leave the rest to God. There are absolutely a lot of things you can do despite those that are out of your control. Focus on that which you can control and give it your best. Focus on your gift or talents and skills that you have to weather the storms instead of just giving up because you are overwhelmed.

You are not competing with anyone to fulfil your purpose; it's your own race with yourself. Never focus on what others are doing rather focus on what you are doing and what you want to achieve. The more you focus on what others are doing instead of your own purpose you get distracted from your own purpose. Stay focused and committed on your purpose without having to keep up with anyone. Get out of the competition and focus more on what needs to be done to further your purpose.

For you to stay focused you need to have clearly defined goals that you write down which will help you further your purpose. Your goals should be SMART that is they must be specific, measureable, attainable, and realistic and time bound. Your goals should be daily, weekly and monthly goals. They are a sure way to keep you focused on your purpose if you follow through every goal that you have set. Follow through your goals and if there is anything that is distracting your focus deal with it.

It is said that procrastination is a thief of time; I would rather want to say it is the thief of dreams. The more you procrastinate the more you are distracted by other things than doing what you were supposed to do. Procrastination doesn't just delay you to what you are supposed to do in most cases it will give you more reasons why you shouldn't do it at all. Stop procrastinating and do what needs to be done when it should be done.

For you to follow through your goals and stay focused you need to analyse the progress that you have made. Check the progress that you are making on a daily basis. Eliminate all possible hindrances to achieving your goals. If you don't know how far you have gone it will be hard to know how much is still yet to be accomplished. Keep track of how far you have gone and consistently stay on course. The more you achieve the small day by day goals you set the more focused you become in achieving your ultimate goals which is your purpose. Don't forget to celebrate the small victories.

CHAPTER FIVE

BIBLICAL CHARACTERS
WHO LIVED ON PURPOSE

MOSES

Moses is one man who lived and pursued God's purpose despite the challenges that he faced, he never gave up. When the children of Israel were enslaved in Egypt by Pharaoh, Moses was born an Israelite who was adopted by the Egyptian king's daughter. One day he saw an Egyptian beating up one of the Israelites and he took the matter into his own hands and he killed him. For the fear of persecution he fled Egypt and went to Midian.

Whilst in Midian he got married to a Midianite woman named Zipporah and he was tending his father in law's sheep. God appeared to him in form of a burning bush on Mount Horeb where Moses was tending the sheep. God spoke to him about going back to Egypt and bring his people from bondage. This was Moses's purpose that he was supposed to carry out.

Considering that Moses was a fugitive who had run away from Egypt, his purpose required him to go back to the same place he ran away from. Moses made every kind of excuse that he could in order to avoid his purpose. He told God that he wasn't the right person for the job that he had for him. He mentions that people will never believe that he was sent by God and he was not an eloquent speaker. Moses couldn't believe that God could use him; he never thought that God had a purpose for him.

You might also be having doubts about your purpose God has called you to do for whatever reason you are disqualifying yourself for. God won't choose people for his purpose like people would choose. He doesn't look at your criminal record, eloquence, education, social status or anything you think is of value to be used by God. He chose you for who you are to him and what you can bring to his kingdom. He chose you even with your shortcomings; you are the right person to carry out his assignment. God qualifies those whom he calls.

God assured Moses that he was going to be with him in accomplishing his purpose, "And God said, "I will be with you. And this will be the sign to you that it is I who have sent you: When you have brought the people out of Egypt, you will worship God on this mountain." Exodus 3:12. Indeed God was with Moses, after he returned to Egypt God used the ten plagues to make Pharaoh relent. Many other great things happened through this journey like parting of the red sea, the Ten Commandments and defeating the Amalekites. God was with Moses in fulfilling his purpose until he was taken away by God.

JOSHUA

Joshua succeeded Moses, following his death. Joshua was commanded to carry on with the responsibility of taking the children of Israel to the Promised Land. God said to Joshua, "Be strong and very courageous. Be careful to obey all the law my servant Moses gave you; do not turn from it to the right or to the left, that you may be successful wherever you go. Keep this Book of the Law always on your lips; meditate on it day and night, so that you may be careful to do everything written in it. Then you will be prosperous and successful." Joshua 1:7-8.

The task before Joshua was not any easy one to accomplish he faced different challenges. The people whom he was leading were said to be stubborn and stiff-necked. He faced difficulties in dealing with the people he was leading. He faced giants and fortified cities which he was to conquer. He also came to the flooded Jordan River. All these challenges Joshua faced made his pursuit of purpose sound impossible. Joshua despite of all these challenges he overcame through applying the word of God and believing in its promises.

Joshua was successful in fulfilling his purpose by doing what God had commanded him to do that is following the book of the law. God gave specific guidelines and orders to Joshua that would make him successful in accomplishing his purpose. Likewise, God gives you a specific guideline for fulfilling your purpose. Be strong and courageous and be careful to observe the law in the Bible and observing what it says for you to be successful and prosperous.

ESTHER

Esther's story is a story of God's purpose, bravery, faithfulness and divine timing. Esther's purpose was to save God's people. She was an Israelite born at a time where Israel was in captivity after disobeying God. Her parents were murdered and she was adopted by Mordecai as his daughter. The King gathered virgins in search of a wife and Esther found favour in the eyes of the King. Esther being a foreigner she was advised by Mordecai to keep her true identity as a secret.

Haman the King's advisor become very furious at Mordecai after he defied the orders to bow down to him. Just because of his hatred for Mordecai, Haman plans to kill all the Jewish people in the Persian Empire and the King granted Haman with authority to carry on with plan since he didn't know that his queen was also Jewish.

Mordecai pleaded with Esther and said that, "For if you remain silent at this time, relief and deliverance for the Jews will arise from another place, but you and your father's family will perish. And who knows that you have come to your royal position for such a time as this?" Esther 4:14. God strategically positioned Esther at this time for a purpose. He had placed her in position of power that she would be used as an instrument to save his people.

Esther was the only Jewish person who had a direct contact with the King. She had access to the King and God used that to further his purpose. Esther after hearing about what was going to happen to her people she decided to go before the King. The King had not summoned her to come for months and it was taboo to go before the King without any invitation even if she was his wife. She asked her fellow Jewish people to pray and fast as she prepared to approach the King about having mercy on the Jews. She went on to appear before the King and her wish was granted, the Jewish people were spared from being killed. In fact the King decided to kill Haman the one who had orchestrated the death of the Jewish people.

Likewise, God placed you at your position for such a time as this for a purpose. Everything that has happen is by God's design and to make sure that his purpose is fulfilled. Look for the reason why God placed you in the position you are in and why you had to go through the experiences that you had. Esther faced different challenges in accomplishing her purpose but she resorted to prayer and fasting which made the King soften his heart. When you are faced with difficulties in accomplishing your purpose, pray and fast about it.

DAVID

David is an interesting character who pursued God's purpose to the extent of being regarded the man after God's heart. From a very early age David started pursuing his purpose. While visiting his brothers at a military camp to bring them food, he was disgusted by the fact that the Philistine giant, Goliath, was challenging and defying the Israelites. "Then the Philistine said, "This day I defy the armies of Israel! Give me a man and let us fight each other." 1 Samuel 17:10

Nobody from the Israelites camp dared to take up the challenge of facing this Philistine giant. David took it upon himself to challenge him. "David asked the men standing near him, "What will be done for the man who kills this Philistine and removes this disgrace from Israel? Who is this uncircumcised Philistine that he should defy the armies of the living God?" 1 Samuel 17:26.

David as young as he was, challenged Goliath in the name of the Lord, God and he won the battle against Goliath. "David said to the Philistine, "You come against me with sword and spear and javelin, but I come against you in the name of the Lord Almighty, the God of the armies of Israel, whom you have defied. This day the Lord will deliver you into my hands, and I'll strike you down and cut off your head. This very day I will give the carcasses of the Philistine army to the birds and the wild animals, and the whole world will know that there is a God in Israel." 1 Samuel 17:45-46. He understood that God will give him victory.

David was the least expected to be anointed the King among

the children of Jesse because he was young and tending sheep. As young and despised as he was God had a purpose for him. God always look at the heart, he doesn't qualify people as we would qualify them. David's accomplishments were many as the King, many battles were won, he reunited the nation and people loved him as their King.

JEREMIAH

Jeremiah was considered a weeping prophet considering many accounts of the challenges he faced to carry out his purpose as accounted in the books of Jeremiah and Lamentations. He was called to warn of the destruction and disaster to befall nations including Babylon, and confronting kings and other nations. He also condemned the burning of children as offerings to Moloch and proclaiming the captivity and famine to be faced by the people. He was called in a time where people of God had deviated from God which caused people to withdraw their blessings.

God called Jeremiah when he was still young and did not know how to speak. Jeremiah gave excuses to God about his age and God said, "But the Lord said to me, "Do not say, 'I am too young.' You must go to everyone I send you to and say whatever I command you. Do not be afraid of them, for I am with you and will rescue you, declares the Lord. Then the Lord reached out his hand and touched my mouth and said to me, "I have put my words in your mouth." Jeremiah 1:7-9. God will always equip you with the gifts and the strength you need to fulfil his purpose. When God gives you an assignment it is not about you, but about him. He gives you all the necessary tools for you to be able to carry out the assignment effectively. He did it with Jeremiah the same thing he did with Moses, he can still do it with you too. Never be discouraged for your inability to do something, God will equip you and give you that ability.

APOSTLE PAUL

Apostle Paul also known by his Jewish name Saul of Tarsus was one of the most influential figures. Although he never walked with Jesus, he is considered one the greatest Apostles who had a unique purpose. Paul used his Jewish and Roman background to preach to both groups. He also wrote more books and letters in the Bible than any other apostle with thirteen books in the New Testament attributed to him.

Paul's purpose started off differently from other people. He was named Saul, before his conversation and he persecuted the early disciples of Jesus Christ. He had an encounter with the Lord when he was on his way from Jerusalem to Damascus where he was granted the right to arrest and bring them back to Jerusalem. The Lord appeared to him in a great light and he was struck blind for three days.

God instructed Ananias to go and heal Paul which was a difficult task for him knowing how much he was persecuting believers. God assured Ananias that he had chosen Paul for a purpose of proclaiming the gospel to both gentiles and Jews. "Lord," Ananias answered, "I have heard many reports about this man and all the harm he has done to your holy people in Jerusalem. And he has come here with authority from the chief priests to arrest all who call on your name." But the Lord said to Ananias, "Go! This man is my chosen instrument to proclaim my name to the Gentiles and their kings and to the people of Israel. I will show him how much he must suffer for my name." Acts 9:13-16.

God called Paul to be an instrument to proclaim the good news about Christ whom he was prosecuting people for to both Gentiles and Jews. Paul was also showed how much he was going to suffer for the sake of God's name. Indeed Paul the prosecutor became the prosecuted. All this was part of God's purpose for Paul's life. He wrote so many epistles encouraging Christians to endure challenges, rejoicing when faced with challenges and being content with the hardships. He made an interesting comment saying, "For our light and momentary troubles are achieving for us an eternal glory that far outweighs them all. So we fix our eyes not on what is seen, but on what is unseen, since what is seen is temporary, but what is unseen is eternal." 2 Corinthians 4:17-18

Paul's purpose was not easy in any way, it was filled with ups and downs, prosecutions and suffering but He kept on pressing towards the goal. You might face difficulties and challenges as you pursue God's purpose for your life, never let the challenges deter you from pressing towards the ultimate goal. In trials and tribulation keep doing what you were called to do and never up.

TIMOTHY

Timothy was a mentee to Paul whom Paul met during his missionary journey who later become his companion together with Silas. Timothy in many occasions travelled with Paul and he carried out some of the important assignments. He was called at a very young age and Paul at one point in time encouraged him to not be discouraged because people said he was young. "Don't let anyone look down on you because you are young, but set an example for the believers in speech, in conduct, in love, in faith and in purity." 1 Timothy 4:12.

Paul imparted the spiritual gifts by laying hands on Timothy. Paul said to Timothy, "Do not neglect your gift, which was given you through prophecy when the body of elders laid their hands on you." 1 Timothy 4:14. When Timothy was prayed for by the elders the Holy Spirit came upon him and he received a spiritual gift. He then became a proclaimer of the good news even in his young age.

Timothy received his spiritual gift which was also what Paul stresses that we all possess our own gift that we received from God. Paul writes, "I wish that all of you were as I am. But each of you has your own gift from God; one has this gift, another has that." 1 Corinthians 7:7. You have your won spiritual gift that God has gifted you that is unique to yourself. Living on purpose is discovering and living that gift. God created you for a purpose and he wants you to fulfil that purpose irrespective of your age. Timothy was young but he was also used by God in witnessing the good news to many.

CLOSING WORD

You are not on earth by accident you were intentionally and strategically positioned for a special purpose. God has created you for a purpose which is bigger than yourself. God's purpose for your life is for you to have a deeper relationship with him while serving others positively impacting them with your talents and gifts you have. In pursuing and fulfilling purpose you will find enlightenment and meaning, success and happiness, and life becomes worth living.

Pursuing God's purpose isn't going to be easy; there are some difficulties that you will face along the way. Just like all the patrons of faith who walked in faith before us like Moses, Joshua, Abraham, David and Paul, only to mention a few but had to face different challenges in fulfilling their purpose. Their success stories is not without challenges but they never gave up even when push came to shove. They kept their faith in God, with their minds fixed on the promises of God and doing everything possible to fulfil their purpose.

God who started the good work in you is always faithful to see it through to completion. He is the one who created you for a purpose and if you rely on him, he will make sure that you have everything you need to fulfil it. Have faith in God, face all your fears with faith and self-confidence. Stay focused, persistent and consistent until you realise your purpose. Defeat is only but a temporary condition; only giving up makes it permanent. Never give up in fulfilling your purpose.

Made in the USA
Columbia, SC
26 May 2020

98419428R00048